A Note to Parents and Caregivers:

With a focus on math, science, and social studies, *Read-it!* Readers support both the learning of content information and the extension of more complex reading skills. They encourage the development of problem-solving skills that help children expand their thinking.

 The PURPLE LEVEL presents basic topics and objects using high frequency words and simple language patterns.

 The RED LEVEL presents familiar topics using common words and repeating sentence patterns.

 The BLUE LEVEL presents new ideas using a larger vocabulary and varied sentence structure.

 The YELLOW LEVEL presents more challenging ideas, a broad vocabulary, and wide variety in sentence structure.

 The GREEN LEVEL presents more complex ideas, an extended vocabulary range, and expanded language structures.

 The ORANGE LEVEL presents a wide range of ideas and concepts using challenging vocabulary and complex language structures.

When sharing a content focused book with your child, read to find out facts and concepts, pausing often to restate and talk about the new information. The realistic story format provides an opportunity to talk about the language used, and to learn about reading to problem-solve for information. Encourage children to measure, make maps, and consider other situations that allow them to apply what they are learning.

There is no right or wrong way to share books with children. Find time to read and share new learning with your child, and pass on the legacy of literacy.

Adria F. Klein, Ph.D.
Professor Emeritus
California State University
San Bernardino, California

Editor: Shelly Lyons
Designer: Abbey Fitzgerald
Page Production: Michelle Biedscheid
Art Director: Nathan Gassman
Associate Managing Editor: Christianne Jones
The illustrations in this book were created with acrylics.

Picture Window Books
5115 Excelsior Boulevard
Suite 232
Minneapolis, MN 55416
877-845-8392
www.picturewindowbooks.com

Printed in the United States of America.

Library of Congress Cataloging-in-Publication Data
Blaisdell, Molly, 1964-
Up, up in the air / by Molly Blaisdell ; illustrated by Ronnie Rooney.
p. cm. — (Read-it! readers: science)
ISBN 978-1-4048-4220-5 (library binding)
[1. Kites—Fiction. 2. Aerodynamics—Fiction.] I. Rooney, Ronnie, ill. II. Title.
PZ7.B542Up 2008
[E]—dc22   2007032921

Up, Up in the Air

by Molly Blaisdell
illustrated by Ronnie Rooney

Special thanks to our advisers for their expertise:

Paul R. Ohmann, Ph.D.
Associate Professor of Physics
University of St. Thomas, St. Paul, Minnesota

Adria F. Klein, Ph.D.
Professor Emeritus, California State University
San Bernardino, California

PICTURE WINDOW BOOKS
Minneapolis, Minnesota

During spring break, Jamar saw an ad in the newspaper. The ad read, "Kite Flying Contest—Saturday." Jamar showed his dad the ad.

"That sounds fun," said Dad.

"I'm going to enter that contest," said Jamar.

Dad looked over Jamar's shoulder. "The rules say you have to make the kite yourself," he said. "How will you do that?"

"I need to find a plan to make a kite," said Jamar. "I had better go to the library."

At the library, Jamar found some books about kites. "Wow, I didn't know there were so many kinds," he said.

"What kinds?" asked Dad.

"Diamonds, delta flyers, sleds, and here's one called a dragon. I don't know which one to pick," said Jamar.

"It's probably best to keep the kite simple," said Dad.

Jamar flipped through the pages and stopped. "This is the one," he said as he pointed to the page.

"Good choice!" said Dad.

"Let's check out this book," said Jamar. "Then I need to make a supply list."

"We can get supplies at the craft store," said Dad.

"Great!" said Jamar. He started writing down everything he would need.

At the store, Jamar checked the list he had made at the library.

Supply List
- one wooden dowel 2 and a half feet
- one wooden dowel 3 feet long
- glue
- string
- ruler
- one small metal ring
- long strip of cloth
- cloth scraps
- poster paint

Jamar and his dad wheeled the cart through the aisles. They found everything on the list.

"It's all here," Dad said. "And we have cloth at home."

"Let's go home, and I'll get right to work," said Jamar.

At home, Jamar followed the plan in his library book. First, he built the frame. Jamar's dad cut notches in the end of each dowel. A dowel is a round rod or stick.

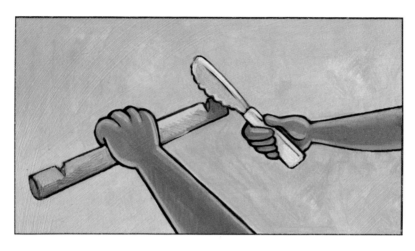

Next, Jamar measured the dowels. The longer dowel would run up and down the kite. The shorter dowel would run from left to right across the kite.

Using a ruler, he measured the length of the shorter dowel and marked its center. He also measured the longer dowel and made a mark that was 8 inches from the top.

He tied the two sticks together at the marks with string. The place where the dowels crossed had to be very tight. He also put glue on that spot.

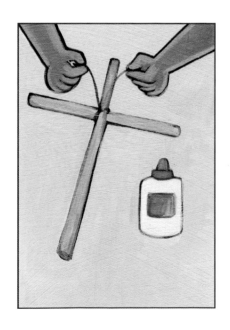

The next day, Jamar used string to add guidelines to the kite frame. The string was strung tightly through each notch on the ends of the dowels.

"Your frame looks great," said Dad.

14

"It's time to cut out the covering," said Jamar. He used the frame as a pattern. He cut two diamond-shaped coverings. He glued the pieces together over the frame, so the frame was completely covered.

After the glue was dry, Jamar was ready to finish the kite.

"What's next?" asked Dad.

"I'll paint it. Then, I'll add the bridle and tail," said Jamar.

A diamond-shaped kite needs four string lines—one line from each point. The four lines meet at a metal ring. The lines from the points to the ring form the bridle.

First, Jamar painted a tiger on both sides of his kite.

Then he attached a string to each corner of the kite. Next, he attached all four strings to the metal ring, making the bridle.

Last, he measured three cloth strips for the tail. He tied cloth scraps at even spaces along the tail.

The next day at the beach, Jamar asked, "Did you know that airplanes are a lot like kites?"
"How is that?" asked Dad.

"Airplanes and kites are heavier than air," said Jamar. "They need something to lift them into the air. Airplanes use engines, and kites use wind."

Lift is the upward force that causes an object to fly. The movement of wind over the surfaces of the kite causes lift.

At the beach, a steady breeze blew. A sailboat raced in the water.

Jamar knew this kind of wind was perfect for kite flying. Too much wind would break the kite. Too little wind, and the kite would not fly.

Jamar put his back to the wind. The breeze would lift his kite.

He carefully let out some string, but the kite fell to the ground.

"It's OK," said Jamar. "I know what to do. The tail is causing too much drag on my kite. I need to make it shorter."

He snipped off part of the tail.

Jamar put his back to the wind again. He let out some line. The kite went up, but not very far.

Drag is the force created by wind pushing on an object's surface. This force slows down the object.

"I'm going to have to adjust one of the strings," Jamar said. "That will change the angle of the kite. The kite will have more lift."

"Wow," said Dad. "You have learned a lot about kites."

"I have," said Jamar. He shortened the longest bridle string by a little.

Jamar put his back to the wind. The breeze hit the kite. Jamar let out some string. This time, the kite shot up in the air.

The next day was the contest. Jamar and Dad went back to the beach. The contest was about to begin. Many kids were testing their kites.

After a few tries, Jamar had the bridle and tail adjusted. He put his back to the wind. He let out some line. His kite bobbed, then it shot upward. It was higher than some kites, but not as high as others.

Soon the judges came by. They looked for the best kite made by a child. They judged design, creativity, and flight.

28

"I can tell you worked hard on this kite," said one judge.

"I did," said Jamar. He smiled with pride.

Soon the judges announced who won.
Jamar's kite didn't win, but he still had fun.
   "I'm sorry," said Dad.
   Jamar was a little disappointed. "It's OK,"
said Jamar. "I still love kite flying."

Activity: Trash Bag Kite

What you need:

- one heavy-duty trash bag
- one 12-inch (30.5-centimeter) stick (bamboo skewers work well as sticks)
- one 8-inch (20.3-cm) stick
- one drinking straw
- packaging tape
- kite string
- a pen
- scissors

What you do:

1. Find the midpoint of the short stick and mark it. Measure 2 inches (5.1 cm) from the top of the long stick and mark it.
2. Cut open the trash bag so it is one sheet of plastic.
3. Tape the long stick to the trash bag.
4. Match the marks and tape the short stick to the trash bag, forming a crossing point with the sticks.
5. Cut out a kite shape using the stick frame as a guide.
6. Snip the end of a straw to make a bridle ring, and cut four 12-inch (30.5-cm) pieces of kite string.
7. Attach a string to each corner of the kite.
8. Attach each of the strings to the straw ring.
9. Cut several 4- or 5-foot (1.2- or 1.5-meter) plastic strips from the remaining bag.
10. Tape these strips to the bottom of the kite for a tail.

How high does your kite fly? Add weight to the tail by taping on a penny. Try adjusting the bridle. Does your kite fly higher? Is it more stable?

Glossary

bridle—the strings that come from the points of the kite; directs the face of the kite at the proper angle to the wind for lift
delta flyer—a kite shaped like a triangle with no tail
diamond kite—a kite with a diamond shape
drag—the force of air that pushes on an object's surface and slows it down
dragon kite—a kite that has a plate-shaped face and an extremely long tail
kite—an object that flies and is made of a light frame that is covered with paper, plastic, or cloth
lift—the upward force of air that causes an object to fly
tail—a group of streamers or one long strip that weighs down the kite; helps the kite be more stable in the wind
wind—moving air

To Learn More

More Books to Read

Branley, Franklyn M. *Air Is All Around You*. New York: HarperCollins, 2006.

Meiani, Antonella. *Air*. Minneapolis: Lerner Publications Co., 2003.

Parker, Steve. *The Science of Air: Projects and Experiments with Air and Flight*. Chicago: Heinemann Library, 2005.

On the Web

FactHound offers a safe, fun way to find Web sites related to topics in this book. All of the sites on FactHound have been researched by our staff.

1. Visit *www.facthound.com*
2. Type in this special code: 1404842209
3. Click on the FETCH IT button.

Your trusty FactHound will fetch the best sites for you!

Look for all of the books in the *Read-it!* Readers: Science series:

Friends and Flowers (life science: bulbs)
The Grass Patch Project (life science: grass)
The Sunflower Farmer (life science: sunflowers)
Surprising Beans (life science: beans)

The Moving Carnival (physical science: motion)
A Secret Matter (physical science: matter)
A Stormy Surprise (physical science: electricity)
Up, Up in the Air (physical science: air)